D1010627

The TRUTH

Diary of a Gutsy Tween

I'M A GIRL, I'M SMART,
AND I KNOW
EVERYTHING!

The TRUTH

Diary of a Gutsy Tween

DR. BARBARA BECKER HOLSTEIN

Sky Pony Press
New York

Sky Pony Press books may be purchased in bulk at special discounts for sales promotion, corporate gifts, fund-raising, or educational purposes. Special editions can also be created to specifications. For details, contact the Special Sales Department, Sky Pony Press, 307 West 36th Street, 11th Floor, New York, NY 10018 or info@skyhorsepublishing.com.

Sky Pony® is a registered trademark of Skyhorse Publishing, Inc.®, a Delaware corporation.

Visit our website at www.skyponypress.com.

10 9 8 7 6 5 4 3 2 1

Manufactured in China, March 2014
This product conforms to CPSIA 2008

Library of Congress Cataloging-in-Publication Data is available on file.

Cover design by Victoria Bellavia
Interior design by Sara Kitchen
Interior illustrations by Julie Matysik

ISBN: 978-1-62873-611-3
Ebook ISBN: 978-1-62914-246-3

Printed in China

“All grownups were children first.
(But few of them remember it.)”

“Grownups never understand anything by themselves, and it is exhausting for children to provide explanations over and over again.”

—From *The Little Prince*

INTRODUCTION

When I was a girl, I knew so many things. I knew a lot of important stuff that my parents and other grown-ups had forgotten. I promised myself that I would find a way to hold on to my knowledge.

Then I grew up and became a teacher and a psychologist. I got married and had children. At work, as a psychologist, I listen to a lot of people's problems—children and grown-ups. I always try to help them. One of the things I do is to point out to them what is right with them, rather than what is wrong. Another thing I do is to teach them how to have more fun. I also help them to remember their own wisdom and the truths that they already know in their hearts.

One day, I decided to find a way to combine what I already knew as a girl with the knowledge I now have as a psychologist. I had to find a fun way to do this that would really help girls and mothers recognize that what we know growing up is just as important as what we learn later in life.

One day, the "girl" just appeared. She knew what to say and how to say it. She did a much better job of sharing *the truth* than I ever could have imagined. So I just let her go for it.

Here is her account of *the truth*. I hope you enjoy it. Remember your promises to yourself when you grow up and don't forget to listen to your kids someday.

I better get out of the way and let the girl begin. . . .

The TRUTH

Diary of a Gutsy Tween

This is my secret diary. Not the one that says "My Special Diary." I leave that around just to fool grown-ups. This is the <u>real</u> truth. This is where I will write everything I don't want to forget, starting tomorrow!

Date: September 19

Dear Diary,

This is the very first page of my new secret diary. So before I begin, here's all you need to know about me:

I am eleven years old.

I live at 100 Maple St.

My school is Riverside Middle School.

I live with my mom, dad, and annoying little brother who is six (only kidding, I really love him).

We have no pets. I hate that. I want a dog!

I am in sixth grade.

My best friend is Angela. We keep secrets.

My other really good friends are Betsy and Gloria.

My teacher is Miss Shannon. I'm not sure I like her.

My favorite books are mystery books. I've recently started reading Nancy Drew, which is an older series but really fun!

My favorite color is pink.

My favorite food is coffee ice cream.

We have a nice house. It has six rooms, a basement, and an attic.

My favorite thing to do on the weekends is read blogs about cooking, crafts, and what other girls my age like to do.

We have two TVs in our house. Our computer is broken, though, so if I want to go online, I have to go to Angela's house, which is a huge pain!

I want something special to happen to me someday, like to win a million dollars.

Date: September 20

Dear Diary,

I am in love. I thought I would fall in love when I was much older, maybe fifteen or sixteen. Not today.

I was sitting in class, reading a chapter in my social studies textbook and trying to answer a stupid question at the end of the chapter. The question was: "Which state has the most coal mines?" Suddenly, the door opened and a new kid walked in.

There he was! I knew as soon as I saw him—he was someone special. He was wearing a cute plaid shirt and he had brown hair and brown eyes.

My heart felt like it turned over in my body. My pulse started to race. I couldn't concentrate on my textbook or the stupid question anymore. I felt excited, like I suddenly had a big secret.

"Our eyes locked."

I once read that in a book that my mom had by her bed. And that's exactly what happened with the new boy—that feeling was true. When I looked into his brown eyes, I felt we had known each other forever. Looking at him made me feel all fluttery inside.

I wanted him to sit near me so badly I could have died. But he sat in the row in front of me, a little to the right. Not too bad. Now I can look at him all day. My best friend, Angela, sits beside him on his right. I hope she doesn't fall in love with him, too. He's mine!

His name is Paul.

Paul

Date: September 21

Dear Diary,

How will I ever be able to think about school and homework again with all these funny feelings in my belly and my heart beating so fast I can't breathe every time I see or think about Paul? From the moment I saw him sitting at his desk when I entered the classroom, I couldn't help but think about him. I could barely concentrate during the spelling test (I'm sure I misspelled almost every word) and I was so busy thinking about Paul holding my hand that I didn't hear the teacher call my name during science. And I just sat and watched him and the other boys play basketball during recess, which Angela thought was strange. She said that I looked like I was in a daze. I didn't want to tell her that I am in love. I feel like I need time to just have this special secret all to myself.

PAUL

I can't wait to go to school tomorrow. Now I know how girls fall in love. I thought it would be a certain way, given what I've read online. Now that it's happened to me, I'm sure how it feels, and I'm only eleven. And that's the truth.

Date: September 28

Dear Diary,

It's been a week now and Paul hasn't even looked at me in school. Well, occasionally he glances in my direction, but nothing all that special. I wish he could see how much I like him and want him to notice me!

I wonder if boys also have the feelings about girls like I have about Paul? I wish my computer at home worked because then maybe I could Google that and see if there are other girls and boys my age who have blogs and who talk about this kind of stuff. I feel nervous to talk about it with my mom—or with anyone, really.

Ugh, I wish Dad would get our computer fixed already! I need some answers! I don't want to Google my questions when I am over at Angela's, though, because I haven't told her yet that I'm in love.

Date: October 12

Dear Diary,

I have a secret.

I want to know about growing up.

I want to ask my mom questions, like when will I need a bra? But I feel like I can't. Whenever I've tried to ask, Mom always looks away and starts to stare at her cell phone. Then she will suddenly "remember" that she has to cook supper or do the laundry and I never really get an answer to my questions. Why is that? Doesn't she know how confused I am and how important this is for me to know? How am I supposed to be ready to get older if she can't even tell me what to expect or when I should get a bra?

Sometimes I wish I was Mrs. Allen's daughter. That's Angela's mom. Mrs. Allen tells Angela everything she needs to know (at least that's what Angela says). And even if Angela has a question her mom doesn't want to answer, Angela can just look it up on her own personal laptop. Angela is so lucky and that's the truth.

I guess I'm a little lucky, though, because

at least I get some of my questions answered secondhand from Angela.

Date: October 13

Dear Diary,

I'm worried. Paul hasn't really said much to me lately but I feel like he's the only boy I'll ever love. All I can think about is our wedding and what kind of dress I'll wear and that we'll live happily ever after like people in the movies. Who will I marry if I don't marry Paul?

How will I ever find another boy to love and how will I ever decide to get married? I don't think I could stand to be alone as a grown-up, and I would die if I couldn't have children. My dolls are my babies now, but someday I'll want real kids.

I've always loved my dolls. I sleep with them still at night, though I don't really admit that to anyone anymore. My favorite doll has holes in her nose and breathes when you press her stomach. I love them so much, but I know I'd love real kids more—someday. But I worry that maybe I'll never have them. And when do you know you want to have kids anyway?

Date: October 14

Dear Diary,

I hate my mom sometimes. We were on the back porch this evening and I finally asked her how I will know that I need a bra? And guess what she did! She just stood up and walked back into the kitchen, saying, "You're too young to be worried about that. I didn't think about things like that at your age. You should be out playing or doing homework. You don't need a bra yet." And that was it. When I went inside, I found her on the phone with her friend.

I knew I shouldn't have bothered. Maybe Angela can ask her mom for me? I feel so angry right now. I hope I can sleep tonight.

Why can't my mom just talk to me and answer my simple questions?

!!!

Date: October 20

Dear Diary,

Yesterday my dad's cousin, George, came to visit us from Las Vegas where he lives. He stayed for lunch and then we took him to the lake and then we all went out to dinner. My parents said it was their treat.

After we came home, we all sat in the living room for a long time. George talked and talked. That would have been okay, except he swore the whole time. He'd say a few words and then he would mix in a swear word. I can't even write them here—you'll just have to believe me. For example, he said, "And what the h— do you think of that, Edith?" My mom just answered as if he hadn't sworn, which was strange because she usually hates swearing and the one time I accidently said a curse word, she grounded me for a whole evening! But she didn't even seem to bat an eyelash when George swore. Then he would go on and swear again and no one would say anything!

Every time George swore, it gave me a bad feeling in my stomach, like I get when I hear people swearing on a YouTube video or in a movie. I finally got up the courage and asked him not to swear anymore, but he just laughed at me and kept talking.

But the truth is I know more than he does. Swearing makes the whole room feel heavy, as if little arrows are being shot off, hitting people and hurting them. Either he doesn't know the truth or he doesn't care. I finally excused myself and came up here to be alone. Sometimes that's better when someone is making you feel uncomfortable. Sometimes I come upstairs when my parents are fighting and just hide in my room. I wish they got along better. I love when they hug each other. Then I feel safe and warm, too.

Date: October 21

Dear Diary,

When I got up this morning, George had already left. And I was glad. At breakfast, I told my mom and dad that I didn't understand why George swore so much. But they didn't seem that bothered and just told me, "That's George."

What happens to grown-ups that they don't seem to care about things like this? Don't they feel bad inside when they hear people saying those bad words?

Grown-ups say they know so much about life, but I'm pretty sure I know more than they do. I know swearing can make people feel bad and that we shouldn't do it. And that's the truth.

Date: October 22

Dear Diary,

Did you know that I'm not afraid to talk to others—not even to people I've never met before. One day, my mom and I were at a restaurant downtown and I had just ordered a delicious cheeseburger with french fries. Across the room, I saw a man wearing an important looking suit who I recognized. He was the boss where my dad works, so I just jumped out of my seat, left Mom, and went up to him. I knew my mom wasn't going to go over to him. She's shy most of the time.

I said, "Hi," told him who I was, and held out my hand for him to shake it.

He smiled such a giant smile and told me that he was happy I had come over to say hello. He offered to walk me back, and when we approached, he said to Mom, "My, what a bright, friendly child you have."

I was so happy with myself. My heart was beating fast and I knew that when I was a grown-up, I would be outgoing all the time, friendly, and not afraid to meet new people.

Date: October 25

Dear Diary,

Today was the best day ever. Dad took us on one of our Mystery Rides. I love them. We get in the car after lunch, switch off the GPS, and then we each get turns directing him. I had the first turn, so I said, "Go straight for two miles." And then Mom said, "Take a right, a left, a right, and a left, and then go straight for one mile." Then my brother said, "Make a left and three rights." I thought it was kind of cute when he said that. He still confuses his left with his right, so who knows if Dad actually turned the way he wanted him to. We kept taking turns and laughing our heads off as we drove by odd places. We passed the city dump, the hospital, and lots of funeral homes, and we ended up in a big park in the center of town.

Finally, Dad called time-out. Then he took over the game and told us to close our eyes and wait until he told us to open them. And when we did, we were near our house, at a tiny store that has the best ice cream cones. So we all got out, went inside, and ate ice cream. I got a coffee cone with sprinkles—my favorite. It was delicious!

The best times are the fun times, when no one is fighting and we all get turns and we all get treats. And that's the truth!

Date: October 26

Dear Diary,

My brother is so dumb. This afternoon he started to cry without any reason. I asked him why he was crying and he told me that he thought that he was the only one who saw colors inside his eyes when he closed them. He said, "I thought I was special."

But today he found out that Billy down the street sees lots of colors when he closes his eyes, too.

All I could think of was how dumb a six-year-old can be. How could he get so worked up over something so silly? Usually he's upset about real things, like not being able to play video games after supper and stuff like that.

But I looked at him and saw how sad he was, so I decided not to be mean to him about it. I just gave him a hug, got him a Kleenex, and brought him a cupcake from the kitchen.

After all, I am his big sister and was once little and sad about silly things, too.

Date: November 1

Dear Diary,

Why does Betsy hate me? I used to think we were good friends. I guess I was wrong.

She is always so mean to me. I think she talks about me behind my back. In fact, I'm sure of it, and I know she is not saying nice things. I even read something on her Facebook page once that I'm pretty sure was about me, though she didn't name any names. And once I saw her point at my skirt and laugh at the same time. Then the other girls who were standing with her started to laugh, too. I looked down at my skirt and thought, "Maybe I grew this year and my skirt is a tiny bit short? Or maybe it was a little faded from being washed a lot?" I felt awful after that.

And to top it off, today her big brother pushed me on the playground for no good reason. I fell backward and hit my head on the metal post of the swing set. I heard Betsy laughing as I got up, with tears falling down my cheeks. I had to stay in the nurse's office with an ice bag on my head for the rest of the afternoon. And my head still hurts a little.

They hate me. Well, I hate them, too!

My mom told me to ignore them. I'm trying to, but they make me feel like I have cooties, like something is wrong with me, every time I am near them.

cooties?

I want to have lots of friends, but it's hard when people are mean to you for no reason. I think I'm going to de-friend Betsy tonight if I go over to Angela's house. I don't need to see her mean comments anymore, and she clearly doesn't think of me as a good friend to her.

The truth is people shouldn't make fun of you. It really hurts.

Date: November 4

Dear Diary,

Since I'm eleven, my mom now lets me catch the bus two blocks from my house and go downtown—all by myself. And I'm not afraid. Mom told me to sit near the driver, and I do. I talk to him sometimes. Other times I read.

Today, on my way downtown, I read the saddest part of Little House on the Prairie—a book I've read a million times and still love! The Ingalls' dog turned around three times and then lay down in his bed and died. I started crying on the bus, which was a little embarrassing, especially since I knew it was going to happen. I was glad I had a tissue with me to blow my nose. At one point, the driver turned around and asked if I was okay, and I told him that I was—that the book had made me sad because the dog died. He smiled in a kind way.

When I got downtown, I bought some barrettes and sweet-smelling hand lotion at the drugstore. Then I got hungry, so I went next door to the ice cream shop and got an ice cream

LOTION

sundae. This time I got marshmallow sauce instead of whipped cream. It's the same price, and I thought it would be a nice change. And it was!

Then, I went back to the drugstore. Next I looked at the makeup. The store downtown has two aisles filled with lipstick, mascara, nail polish, and lots of other things that I see my teacher, my mom, and other women wear. I wonder when I should start wearing these things? Maybe next time I'm in town, I should buy some mascara instead of a sundae.

Drugstores are great because there are so many things to look at and buy in them. If you get tired looking in one aisle, you can always find another aisle to wander down. I think I spent a good half hour just wandering around the store. And if you have to go to the bathroom, there's one right there, too. But I kept thinking about the makeup and have decided I'll buy some the next time I'm there.

The same bus driver was at the wheel when I got on the bus to go back home. It made me happy to see him again. I'm so glad I can do things by myself. I feel so grown-up when I do.

I don't think grown-ups understand how important it is to do things on your own and not be treated like a baby. I am smart and I have a brain. I'm lucky my mom and dad let me do a lot on my own—have a Facebook page, travel downtown by myself, help cook, etc. I have a friend named Shannon. Her parents are very rich, but she never gets to go downtown by herself. She can't believe that my parents let me! Shannon and her family live on my street, but they are moving away next month to a house with ten rooms! Her mom drives her everywhere, but I feel sorry for her. She doesn't seem very happy.

The truth is parents should let their kids do things for themselves when they are old enough.

Date: November 7

Dear Diary,

My brother and I had to go sleep at my cousin Larry's house last night. My parents had to go out to some sort of dinner event for Dad's work. Instead of getting a babysitter (or letting me stay with my brother at home alone), they think it's easiest to just leave us with Aunt June and Uncle Joe. But I really don't like being at their house, especially if Larry is home. He teases me, won't share his computer, and is not very nice. I don't know why he thinks he can tease me just because I'm six years younger than he is.

Once, when I was younger, Larry told me that my spaghetti was really worms. I almost threw up. He can be a jerk sometimes.

The good news was that he was out late at a basketball game. We didn't even see him except at breakfast and then he tried to trip me as I walked by him. He is so stupid and childish.

My brother and I fell asleep in the basement bedroom with the TV on. That was fun. We shared a big old double bed they keep down there. Aunt June made us popcorn and let us eat it in bed. I loved cuddling up next to my brother and munching popcorn.

Today, I asked my mom why Larry is so annoying and mean to me. My mom said, "Maybe he's that way because he doesn't get enough attention from his parents."

I really don't care why he's that way, to be honest. He shouldn't make fun of me and try to trip me when I walk by him. It's not right.

Date: November 10

Dear Diary,

There is a secret thing I do with my body. I can't help it. It feels so good.

I get a lot of scabs on my knees from rollerblading and falling a lot. In the beginning, the scab is really hard and sticks to my skin for a long time. But the day comes when it starts to feel a little loose, and that's when I can't stop checking it. I'm waiting for just the right day when the scab is almost ready to fall off. That's the day I pick it, and I love that feeling as it comes off my skin.

My brother says this is gross. But it's the truth! I really like that feeling.

And here's a secret about when I grow up: I am going to have two monkeys, two horses, two dogs, two cats, and two birds. Oh, and I forgot, six kids.

But right now, I just want a dog. Mom and Dad said no, but I'm going to keep trying to badger them until they have to say yes.

Date: November 14

Dear Diary,

I think I just solved another mystery in a Nancy Drew book. I'll finish the book later. I'm so glad the librarian at school, Miss Manning, suggested Nancy Drew to me. At first, the books looked kind of old-fashioned and not as exciting as the other vampire series and fantasy series my friends like to read. But once I read the first Nancy Drew mystery, I realized how exciting they are. I just love how smart she is, and I've realized that I like trying to solve the mysteries, too—and I'm actually pretty good at it. This book makes twenty-seven Nancy Drew mysteries that I've read in my whole life. I think that's pretty cool.

Whenever I read these mysteries, I remind myself that I am smart! Most of the time, I solve the mystery way before the end of the book—but I still like to see how Nancy figures it out. She has such a cool life in these books.

I'd like to have a life like hers when I'm seventeen. She gets to do all sorts of stuff by herself. She has a great boyfriend. He is handsome and in love with her. And she has a maid! The maid makes such good food and Nancy is always dressed in such pretty clothing. I think having a maid might be a little bit overkill, but I would like to eat fancy food and wear beautiful clothes every day.

I've decided that being smart and pretty are important to me.

Date: November 18

Dear Diary,

I don't always think I'm pretty. I don't look like the movie stars I see online, or the girls in the teen magazines. When I stand next to my cousin Sandra, I don't feel pretty at all. She has perfect everything (hair, face, clothes), and it isn't fair. Once we had a picture taken together. There Sandra was with perfect bangs, shiny hair, a wide movie-star smile, and straight posture. And there I was with messy hair and a slanted smile, and I was not standing up straight at all. I felt a little jealous of Sandra. My aunt printed out a copy for each of us to keep, but I didn't keep mine. I ripped it up when I got home.

Mom told me she thought I looked cute in the picture when she checked her email on her cell phone. I didn't really answer, and she went right on to her next email.

Sometimes I stand in front of the bathroom mirror and look at myself. When I do that, I feel pretty. I have dirty blond hair and brown eyes. My teeth are a little crooked and I have a space between my top two front teeth, but my mom says that makes my smile interesting. I also think I have nice hands. They look good in the mirror, too. Sometimes I hold up my hands in the mirror, like I'm in a commercial selling nail polish. I just kind of smile at myself and hold my hand up so the nails show and my eyes shine. Then I move my hand a little, like models do on TV. I really feel special when I'm doing this.

I like looking at myself when I'm alone. That's when I feel the most pretty.

Date: November 20

Dear Diary,

The past few days, I've been thinking a lot about looks and I've decided something: the most important thing you can do is to <u>feel</u> pretty. If you feel pretty, then you look pretty. That is the truth for me.

After weeks and weeks of pining away for him, today Paul looked right at me. He made me feel really good about myself—really pretty—when he did that. And then he smiled. He was wearing a green sweater. I wish I could hug him and hold hands with him like we were really a couple.

I think I'm in love with him even more now. I just wish I knew what to do about it. Should I tell him I am in love with him? What if he just walks away from me or looks confused? I would die of embarrassment. Maybe it's time to tell Angela about my feelings. I have wanted to a hundred times, but then I get cold feet. She might think I am silly. I've got to figure out something.

That's it. I'm going to call her now before I lose the nerve to do it. I just hope she doesn't make fun of me for liking a boy.

i ♡ paul

Date: November 21

Dear Diary,

Angela was really nice to me when I told her about my crush on Paul and how much I am in love with him. She told me that she actually has a crush on Greg and might be in love with him, too. We laughed a lot on the phone until my dad made me hang up and go to bed. I'm so happy that Angela knows my secret. Maybe we can figure out what to do about our crushes together.

Today, I was bored in math class, so I started to think about the million ways I know to have fun: hanging out with friends, shopping for clothes, playing games online, taking pictures in photo booths, rollerblading. But one way not to have fun is to be picked last for kickball! That makes me feel rotten. I hate standing there on the playground, knowing that each time a name is called I'm closer to being the last person picked for a team. And it's all Chris and Billy's fault, really. The teacher always picks them as the team captains, though I don't know why. I see the gleam in their eyes as they size up who the good players are. They are so mean. Don't they ever think about how I feel, standing there with fewer and fewer kids to protect me from the truth that I can't kick the ball so well? I know I'm not the best player, but sometimes it would be nice to be picked first—or at least near the beginning. I hate them.

Sometimes I just want to quit school and become a sales person in the toy department of a department store. But Mom says I can't quit school—that it's against the law, in fact. You have to be at least sixteen before you can leave school. And if I'm really honest, I think that by that time, maybe I'll have forgotten all about kickball.

Date: November 22

Dear Diary,

We played kickball again today and again, Billy and Chris picked everyone else before me. I was left alone on Chris's team this time, and I saw him roll his eyes when he saw that I would have to be on his team. I guess it's a good thing I have ways to have fun that don't depend on mean kids like Billy and Chris.

I have lots of fun when I pedal really fast on my bike downhill. When I do that, I stand up on the pedals and my hair blows behind me. I imagine I'm a circus rider standing up on her horse, except I'm on a bike.

I rollerblade, too. I can rollerblade for a long time, even longer than I ride my bike. I love the sensation of gliding down the street. I feel like a figure skater.

But the best thing in the whole world, whether I rollerblade or ride my bike, is the feeling I get when I finish. If I'm not in a rush to get inside for dinner or something, I take a moment to sit down on the curb and smell the skin on my arms. I love the smell after all that exercise. It smells like fresh earth. Sometimes I even lick it. It tastes nice and salty. Of course, this is my secret. Kids would probably make fun of me if they knew the truth about licking my sweaty skin.

Date: December 1

Dear Diary,

Last night my parents had a big fight. I could sort of hear what they were saying through the wall of my room. My eyes were shut tight, but my ears were wide open, like elephant ears, trying to hear every word. I couldn't, but they made me nervous and I couldn't sleep. So today in school I was really tired.

This morning I asked my brother if he heard anything last night, and he said no. But that doesn't surprise me. He is only six and sleeps like a log. I'm the one that ends up staying up late, worrying about my parents' fighting, with my heart pounding so loudly that I keep thinking it is going to pop out of my chest.

Mom and Dad are the grown-ups. They shouldn't have stupid fights that keep their daughter awake. And anyway, fighting never seems to solve anything, and even Mom told me that fighting isn't a good way to handle your problems. No one feels better after being yelled at or put down. No one is going to cooperate any better just because you yell at them and tell them all the things they do are wrong. Even I know that!

And besides, they ruined my sleep. I thought parents were supposed to make sure their kids got lots of rest, so we can grow. I don't think it's nice of them to keep me awake. I should be fast asleep in bed, having sweet dreams. That's another thing I know.

I could teach my mom and dad so much if only they would listen. Why do they seem to want to put each other down? I don't get it. They waste so much time fighting, and before you know it, everyone's feeling sad or angry and the day (or night) is ruined.

This is one thing I'm really promising myself never to do! My dad says, "Don't make a mountain out of a molehill." Well, even though he forgets his own words, I'm going to remember them. I'm going to try to never fight over stupid things. I will talk about my problems and try not to yell. And that's the truth.

Date: December 5

Dear Diary,

It's official. I hate Angela.

She just told me that her parents are buying a new business in upstate New York and that she'll be moving soon. Well, as far as I'm concerned, the sooner it happens the better. Yesterday she had the nerve to sit next to Paul in art even though there were other empty seats in the room. She kept laughing and talking to him, when she knows how much I love him and want to ask him to be my boyfriend. How could she do that to me? We're supposed to be best friends! The whole day in school I had to watch her flirt with him, and I felt like I was dying.

I said something to her at lunch, and she acted all innocent, saying, "What are you talking about? We were just talking about the science project." But I know she's lying. She was flirting with him and is no longer my best friend. Maybe I'll de-friend her tonight if she leaves the room when I'm on her computer.

Date: December 9

Dear Diary,

Paul has been absent for three days. I hope he's not really sick. I miss him so much and each day keep hoping he'll be at his desk when I enter the classroom.

I keep thinking about the hill behind his house. Before Angela started flirting with Paul—before I stopped liking her—she told me that kids go there and play Spin the Bottle. Angela knows everything. The land used to be a place for the Boy Scouts to have outdoor meetings and make a campfire and toast marshmallows. Now Angela said certain kids sit in a circle around where the fire used to be and spin the bottle and kiss each other.

I wonder if Paul knows what goes on up there in the woods behind his house? I wish Paul, me, and the other kids from class could play Spin the Bottle so I could get the chance to show Paul how much I like him.

On second thought, no, I don't. I don't want anyone else to get a chance to kiss him but me.

Date: December 10

Dear Diary,

Gloria is in my dance class. And I hate her. I hate her because her teeth are straight, so she'll never need braces. That isn't fair! Also, her thighs are slimmer than mine and don't have little puckers on them. I hate my puckers. This summer at the beach, my mom told me to just hold my stomach in and no one will notice my legs. But that is <u>not</u> the truth!

The truth is Gloria has nicer legs and she knows it. During our class, she does turns easily, like a real ballerina. And her legs look perfect. Who wouldn't be able to turn so well with those legs? I guess she'll grow up to be a great dancer. I'm sure I won't. I don't turn half as well and my legs are not nearly as long and perfect.

I think I'll trip her by accident when she walks by me the next time in school when I just happen to be stretching my leg as she walks by my desk.

Date: December 16

Dear Diary,

Sometimes, on the weekend, I like to put on fashion shows in front of the bathroom mirror. I get out some of my mom's clothes and model them like the real models I've seen on the TV or online. Of course, I make sure my mom isn't home when I do this. She's probably tell me I was being vain, whatever that means.

Yesterday, I took Mom's beautiful violet velvet dress with the blue Chinese silk shawl that our cousin brought her from her trip to China and snuck into the bathroom. I put on her high heels and her dangling earrings, the ones she told me Dad gave her the day I was born. Then I walked around in front of the mirror like I was a princess. I smiled at myself in the mirror and nodded a little, saying hello to the crowd I imagined would be taking photos and asking for my autograph. It felt so good.

So far my mom doesn't know that I'm taking her things because I'm always careful to put them back exactly where I find them. I don't think she'd like me rummaging through her stuff very much. I know I'd be mad at her if she did that to me, but I can't help it. Sometimes I just like to pretend that I'm someone special.

Date: January 10

Dear Diary,

Today it was raining outside, and I had nothing to do. I got out my old fairy-tale books. I used to read them all the time, but now I only do so once in a while. As I flipped through the tattered pages, I wondered what it would have been like to be Sleeping Beauty. What would it feel like to be asleep so long and then finally be awakened by a prince's kiss? If I were asleep like that, would Paul come along and kiss me? Would he come on a white horse and scoop me up and throw me on the back of the horse and take me to his palace? Would we head deep into an enchanted forest and then he would love me forever? What if he never came? Could I wake myself up? I sure hope so.

My mother is really good at pretending to listen. But I can always tell that she isn't really paying attention. She either looks away or suddenly remembers something that she has to do in another room.

Today, I was trying to talk to her about Paul. I told her I have a crush and his name is

Paul. She looked surprised and said something about how young I still am. Then her cell phone rang and she answered. She never came back to talk to me. I am so mad.

I could teach grown-ups so much if only they would listen. Lots of times they pretend to listen and then they answer you, but they haven't really heard what you said or asked. They think they are off the hook just because they sort of answered you.

But they aren't off the hook.

Date: January 15

Dear Diary,

Why do my parents have to fight over stupid things? I don't get it. Before you know it, everyone's in a bad mood and the day is ruined, like today. Mom and Dad were screaming at each other this morning as my brother and I left to catch the bus. Something about money and my mom being stupid and the checkbook not balancing. I was so glad to leave. So was my brother. We ran to the bus stop. My heart was still pounding on the ride to school.

I remember last summer—there was a day that we never made it to the lake because Dad kept yelling at Mom about a dent in the car and telling her she was stupid for parking the way she did in front of the drugstore. I even heard him say, "Of all the women in the world, I'm married to the stupidest one."

But I think Mom is smart. I remember it made me feel so sick to hear Dad talk like that to Mom. Then Dad had rushed out of the house and took the car, and Mom went into her bedroom and closed the door. I think she was crying.

I remember standing in the hallway with my brother. Both of us were in our bathing suits. I was sweating and cold at the same time. It was an awful feeling.

Date: February 7

Dear Diary,

I know I am very smart and do you know how I know that? Smart people solve mysteries and add numbers quickly and realize if someone is lying. Like I knew Gloria was lying last week when she told me that I was doing so much better turning in dance class. I know she was just trying to make me feel better, but I also know I'm still the worst in the class. And that's the truth.

I wish I could be more like the girls I read about in books—like Nancy Drew and others. I know I'm smart, because in many mystery books, I solve the crime or figure out what happened well before it's revealed in the book. But the girls I read about in books and sometimes online, when we have Internet time at school, seem so smart and have lots of friends and seem really self-confident. I hope that someday—someday soon—I'll feel like that. I guess I can't wait to grow up if it only means I can be completely confident in myself.

Sometimes I wish you could talk to me as I am writing to you. I know that's silly—you are just a diary—but it would be nice to hear what you'd think about all this stuff. It would be cool if we were email pen pals. Then I could write to you and you could write back. Maybe you would be real smart at something too, like solving puzzles or doing Sudoku. I know you can't answer me, but I just want you to know I wish you could.

Date: February 14

Dear Diary,

Today is Valentine's Day. I was so worried when I went to school that I wouldn't get any valentine's cards. There is nothing worse in the world than not getting enough Valentine's Day cards.

But this year it's even worse. Being in love makes Valentine's Day even worse, I think. All I could think about last night lying in bed was what if Paul doesn't give me a valentine? How could I stand it?

I worked last night on my valentine's cards. I made one for each kid in my class. I made Paul's just a tiny bit bigger than the other's, though. Only I would know that I had made his special. So it was my secret.

Miss Shannon decorated our classroom so pretty for our Valentine's Day party. There were hearts pinned up all over the room and she had even put up red and pink streamers. I think she must like Valentine's Day a lot, even though we still had to do our homework.

But, at 2:00 p.m., the class monitor dropped off cupcakes and ice cream

BE MY VALENTINE!

and candy. Then we started our Valentine's Day party. There was a giant box up on the front table with a slot in the top. That's where we put all of our valentine's to be delivered.

Angela, Fred, and Stacey got to empty the box and deliver the valentine's while we all ate our cupcakes and ice cream. And guess what? I got a lot of valentine's! As they were delivered, I kept looking over at Paul. But he didn't look back. He was busy eating. I wondered what he could be thinking about and what he would do when he saw my card to him.

Everyone was laughing and having a good time. Even Miss Shannon was smiling as she opened all the valentine's that we gave her. So I started to open mine. Nothing from Paul. I checked another card. Not from him either. I was feeling a little sick. My heart was pounding.

I got to the last envelope. My heart leapt. It was from Paul! My life was saved. And guess what it read on the front!

It read: "Will you be my Valentine?"

Oh, yes, Paul! I will be your Valentine!

Today was the most perfect, most wonderful day ever!

Date: February 15

Dear Diary,

I was hoping all last night that Paul would treat me differently today, but everything was just the same. Maybe he really didn't mean that he wanted me to be his Valentine. Maybe he just gave me that to be nice. Maybe all the girls got one from him. Maybe his mom was the one who actually filled them out for him.

I want to go and ask him if he meant what was on the card, but I'm afraid to know what he really thinks, especially if he doesn't like me like I like him.

Date: March 14

Dear Diary,

I'm so excited. Today in the mail there was a package for me from Aunt Belinda. She lives in Colorado and I hardly ever see her, but she always remembers me. Last year she sent me this diary that I'm writing in now. I wonder what she sent me this year. Since my birthday is still two weeks away, I'm not going to open the package yet. I think I'll hide it in my underwear drawer. I like to have secrets and I like to solve mysteries, even if I make them up myself!

Now I have a new mystery to solve: "The Mystery of the Unopened Package."

Date: March 15

Dear Diary,

I thought it might be good to make a list of things I know how to do:

(list not finished)

* I know what to do if I find a lost child.
* I know how to earn money. In the winter, I shovel snow for the Bixsters. They are old. In the summer, I sometimes weed the garden for Mrs. Offen.
* I know how to clean the house (but I hate to do it).
* I know how to do laundry (but I hate to do that too).
* I know how to iron and I like to sometimes, especially if I can watch TV at the same time.
* I know how to knit. I made six scarves last winter and four winter hats. Mrs. Miller taught me, and this year she is going to teach me how to make mittens and maybe a sweater. I'm so excited. I love picking out the wool. And it is so relaxing to knit. And when I want to

find a new pattern to try. I am good at Googling that, too.

* I know how to cook grilled cheese and scrambled eggs and how to make pudding.
* I know how to draw pictures of faces. I can also draw horses.
* I know how to get into the house when I forget the back door key. Mom keeps a key on the inside of the door. I have to push it out of the lock onto a piece of newspaper and then wiggle the newspaper under the door until the key slides under the door to the outside.
* I know how to read books that are above my reading level.
* I know how to play the piano and make up music, even though I never took any lessons.
* I know how to help a choking baby or little kid, because I took a special class before I was allowed to babysit.

And here is a list (also not complete) of things I can do really well:

* I can lift my brother and he weighs a lot.

* I can ride my bike for hours and go really fast downhill.
* I can rollerblade and ice skate.
* I can do summersaults and bend over backwards.
* I can dance and make up my own dance moves.

Date: March 16

Dear Diary,

I'm really worried. I think I want to be a ballet dancer when I grow up, but I have trouble turning and that might mean I can't be one. The teacher says that turns are the most important thing for ballet dancers to be able to do. I hope she's wrong. Ever since I was a little girl, I've loved to dance. Whenever Grandma came over I would put on my princess hairband and my tutu skirt and dance for her. She always clapped and then pulled me on her lap and kissed and hugged me. I loved how good I felt. Even now I dance all the time in my room. Except no one watches anymore.

I'm going to try harder like I did with ice skating. I made myself stand on the ice in my ice skates and practice, even with my ankles caving in, until I could skate just like the other kids—and even skate backward.

Date: March 18

Dear Diary,

I saw Paul's mom today for the first time ever. She brought his lunch into the classroom. She looks very nice. She had on lipstick and a really nice sweater. It was blue.

I tried to look really special and nice when she was in the room. I sat up really straight and raised my hand to show that I was a good student. No one else had their hand up. I didn't know what I would say if the teacher called on me (since we weren't asked any questions). But she didn't anyway, so I was safe.

I wonder if Paul's mom noticed me? I hope so! I hope she saw what a smart, pretty, nice girl I was and I hope she tells Paul that he should ask me to be his girlfriend.

Date: March 23

Dear Diary,

Exciting news! I have a new friend. We have tons of fun together. Her name is Dawn and she is in another sixth-grade class, so I've never really spent much time with her before. But we started talking at recess one day and decided we have a lot in common. We've been hanging out for a few weeks now, and she officially called me her friend the other day. So there you have it!

I actually got to sleep over at Dawn's house last night, and we talked until late at night and laughed really hard about all sorts of things.

Her house felt funny compared to mine, though. Her parents don't say much to me and her mom smokes. Their rooms seem darker. I think it's because they have dark curtains on the windows. I don't know what the smell is in the house. It's a little yucky, though.

But I still like to go there because we tell each other secrets and sometimes talk about grown-up stuff, like boys. We even look at each other's chest to see if anything is happening yet, like some of the girls in middle school.

Nothing's happening with my chest, yet, but hopefully soon!

Date: March 24

Dear Diary,

I finished reading Black Beauty yesterday. I've been crying on and off for days while reading it, and as I finished the book, I cried for two hours straight. My nose was so stuffed up, I had to take nose drops just to breathe again. My dad asked me why I was crying so much. I told him it was because the story was very sad and that people are mean to animals.

I asked him why are people so cruel, but he said he didn't really know—that some people just aren't as nice as others. But Black Beauty was such a kind, wonderful horse. How could anyone ever think of making him into soap? I can't stand it! Even though it's only a book, I know people are cruel in real life—to both animals and to each other. I wish I could stop it somehow.

Date: March 26

Dear Diary,

What is wrong with people? I had to read The Diary of Anne Frank in school. Anne died when she was only a few years older than I am. And she loved life so much. How could it be that someone so young was taken away from her home and killed, just because she was seen as different? It doesn't make any sense. And this really happened!

Reading the book made me want to scream out to the whole world, "Stop being mean! Start caring about each other!"

Sometimes I wonder if my parents realize what makes me really sad, like people being mean to animals and the story of Anne Frank. Do they also get saddened by these things? Am I the only one in the whole world who just wants people to be nice to one another? I know my parents love me, but I don't think they really understand what makes me feel so rotten. Maybe parents just can't understand once they grow up. They love their kids but they forget what it feels like to be a kid. I'm going to promise this to myself now: I won't ever forget!

Date: March 27

Dear Diary,

My parents hurt me so much by fighting with each other. I don't really know why they fight, but when I hear Dad say that he is going to take his suitcase out of the closet and go to Grandma's for good, I get really scared and sad. I lie in bed and my heart just pounds. I don't want my dad to leave and not live here anymore. Why would he even say that?

Why do they always seem to fight so late at night, too? How can I get enough sleep to go to school and think about math and spelling and history and all that? How can I concentrate on anything else but worrying that I'll come home and my dad will be gone along with his suitcase?

The truth is that you should try to get along, especially if you say you love someone. My mom and dad put each other down, even sometimes call each other names. It's not right. Why do they do that?

I hope they will stop fighting someday soon.

Date: March 28

Dear Diary,

I still watch Paul all the time at school. I am still sure that this is real love. I imagine us together, swimming and then lying in the sun on a towel and looking into each other's eyes. Even though he doesn't treat me like I am special to him, I think of him all the time. Recently he accepted my request to be Facebook friends and I can see some of his pictures online when I'm at my friends' houses. He looks like he's always having fun with his friends and family.

When I see him in school and get that special feeling of excitement that I never get with anyone else, how can I not daydream about him? Angela told me she daydreams about Greg. She even imagines them living in a camper when they grow up and going cross country with their two babies. She said she will probably have twins, as her mother is a twin. I imagine Paul and me living on a small farm with lots of animals. Maybe we would both be teachers and come home every night and take care of the cows and pigs. I love that daydream.

I know my body will be different someday. Sometimes I stand in front of the mirror and lean over so my chest turns into breasts and I look grown-up. I think I like the thought of that—of looking more adult.

I don't know all the stuff that is going to happen over the next few years, but I do know that I want to marry Paul someday. I can't even begin to think about us not ending up together—our own happily ever after.

Date: March 30

Dear Diary,

Today is my birthday and I'm twelve years old! My grandparents and aunts sent me cards with money inside. I got $100.00 altogether. At first I wanted to get an iPod, but then Mom said no. So I've decided that I'm going to get a new bike with the money and the fifty dollars I already saved. The bike I want is shiny dark blue. My mom said she'd take me to pick it up tomorrow when she gets home from work. I'm so excited. I have never had a bike with more than one speed before. I really feel grown up!

We had my favorite meal tonight: steak. It was really tender and I even got the part with the bone in it. My dad usually takes that part, but since it was my birthday, I got it instead. Then we had cake and ice cream for dessert. Grandma and Grandpa came over for dessert and everyone sang "Happy Birthday" to me. I felt really loved, what with all the hugs and kisses.

While we were eating the cake, Grandma asked if Aunt Belinda had sent me a present. And then I remembered! It was still in my drawer hidden away. I excused myself from the table and ran upstairs. I pulled open my underwear drawer and there it was—the unopened package.

I ripped the paper off the box. I opened the felt lid of the little box and inside was a gold locket on a chain. It was so beautiful and in the shape of a heart. And on the front was an engraved design.

I noticed the small clasp on the locket and opened it. Inside, there were spaces for two pictures. Aunt Belinda had put a picture of me in one of the openings. The other was blank. I love it—it's so beautiful!

Then I read her note, which stated: "To my precious niece. Happy Birthday and many more. Love, Aunt Belinda."

I jumped up and down, holding the locket right up to my heart. Then I put it on before rushing back downstairs to show it off.

Grandma admired the locket and said it was really lovely. When I showed her how it opened and let her glance at my photo inside, she asked. "Who will you put in the other side? Your brother, maybe?" I just gave her a look and said that I'd definitely never put him on the other side.

But it was a good question. Whose picture should I put in the other side?

Date: April 2

Dear Diary,

I'm wearing my locket to school every day. All the girls love it. Even Miss Shannon said how lovely it is. Everyone asked if I had any pictures in it yet. I showed them my picture and said I was still deciding about the other side. A lot of them suggested my brother. That is such a stupid idea. I love him, but I don't want to wear a picture of him with me all the time. Gross!

When we were in the girl's bathroom Angela asked me when I am going to put Paul's picture in the locket. Then we started to laugh and I told her to be quiet. I would die if anyone else heard her. No one in school knows about Paul and me except Angela. Then we heard a toilet flush and my heart started beating so hard. A girl from the first grade came out of the stall and didn't even look at us. I don't think she heard Angela. I was so relieved. Then we just started to laugh again. It felt so good. I love laughing that way. I only do it with Angela. I guess I'm not really mad at her anymore. And I think I'm really going to miss her if she moves away.

Date: April 18

Dear Diary,

Today I was standing in line behind Paul and noticed that we are now the same height. I guess I've grown a lot this year and he hasn't. When I asked Mom about that, she said it's common at my age for girls to start catching up in height to the boys—and sometimes growing taller too.

But the truth is, I liked it when Paul was taller than me. But that hasn't stopped me from loving him, even though he still hasn't asked me to be his girlfriend—he hasn't even written on my Facebook wall, not even for my birthday. I know sometimes boys do ask girls to be their girlfriends even at twelve. My cousin Ann goes to a school where lots of kids have boyfriends and girlfriends in the sixth grade. I don't know anyone around here who does, though. So I don't really expect it to happen.

Date: May 14

Dear Diary,

My world is coming to an end. At lunch, I told Mom again about Paul and how much I love him and that I think I want to get married to him someday. This time she was actually listening to me. And do you know what she told me? She told me not to expect to marry Paul someday. She said I'll meet lots of other boys before I get married. She made me so mad when she said that. Paul is the only boy I'll ever love—I'm sure of it! I don't think she understands that at all.

Every day I know how I feel just by looking at him. He is the smartest boy in the room, and I can't imagine growing up and not being with him. I would rather die.

I am in love!

Date: May 20

Dear Diary,

Today my feelings were hurt.

I usually raise my hand a lot in class, because I have a lot of questions to ask. So today, Miss Shannon was talking about the wheel and how it changed so many things in the world once it was invented. I raised my hand and asked what the world might have been like if something else had been invented instead of the wheel. And then Miss Shannon just looked at me with her really sharp gray eyes and said, "Now, isn't that a silly question!" Then she turned to everyone else and asked them to think of other inventions that depend on the wheel.

I'm sure I turned three different shades of red after that. I mean, I felt bad that Miss Shannon thought my question was dumb. Sometimes she doesn't call on me at all, and I know she sees my hand waving. That makes me feel bad, too. What's so wrong with asking questions? My dad once told me that there are never stupid questions, only stupid answers. So what was so wrong with what I asked her?

But I won't stop raising my hand and asking questions, even if I get a funny feeling in my chest when Miss Shannon ignores me or puts me down.

Date: May 30

Dear Diary,

I think it's time to make a list of the things that grown-ups should remember. This way, when I'm a grown-up, I'll remember them, too:

* Don't be mean to animals.
* Try not to swear.
* Don't fight with anyone you love.
* Don't put people down or call them names.
* Believe your child if she tells you she is in love.
* Answer a kid's questions.
* Listen to their ideas.
* Get your kids a dog when they want one.

Date: June 7

Dear Diary,

The most fun I think I have ever had so far in my life was being in the school play last week. I didn't have the biggest part, but I knew from the time I got my role that I was going to do a great job, and I did.

The way I felt as I said my lines was so wonderful. I could feel my whole body swell as if it got as big as the moon. I could feel the pressure inside of me pushing me to "be" the princess in the story. I knew my connection with her and her feelings would come through.

And they did. I was so good. I knew as the words came out of my mouth that my voice sounded great and my face looked like the princess I was supposed to be, and I knew that afterward people would come up to me and compliment me. And boy, did they!

I was surrounded by everyone—friends, family members, and a few teachers. A few people told me I should be an actress when I grow up. I have to admit: I loved all the attention. My parents even brought me flowers and my dad took my picture with the rest of the cast. And my brother even handed me a rose and he looked so proud of me! I looked good in the picture, in my long dress that was what a princess would wear. But the picture doesn't show how I was flying inside.

I will never forget that night.

Date: June 11

Dear Diary,

I know I would be much prettier if my mom would let me wear makeup. When I was in the school play, I got to wear a long dress and makeup. I could tell by looking at myself in pictures after how makeup makes a big difference. And I really want to wear it now!

I asked Mom why my face looks better with makeup on. She wasn't really listening that well and said something about my sallow skin and black rings under my eyes (which are caused by my allergies). Even though she just said it in passing, I think she must be right. But then why won't she let me wear it? She said I have to wait to wear makeup for at least another year, when I'm a teenager. That's a long time not to look my best.

I wonder if Paul would notice if I wore makeup? I bet he would and I bet he'd ask me to be his girlfriend right away, too. The pretty girls in pictures online and in movies who have boyfriends all wear makeup.

Even Angela gets to wear a little makeup on special occasions. Her mom lets her wear a little blush, some pink lipstick, and even some mascara. Her mom is so with it! What's wrong with my mom? She is still treating me like a little kid!

Thank goodness school is over next week. Last week, Miss Shannon made us do a research project. She said it is good training but didn't say what for. Anyway, we all had to pick a topic and then go to the computer lab and do research online. We could pick from either science or social studies topics. I am sick of social studies. I don't care about the states and what they are famous for. So I picked something to do with science: the weather. I think that is an interesting topic.

We used the Internet and online encyclopedias to research the project. We couldn't just copy what was said in them, though. We had to put each fact down in our own words. That was really hard, but I think I did an okay job with it.

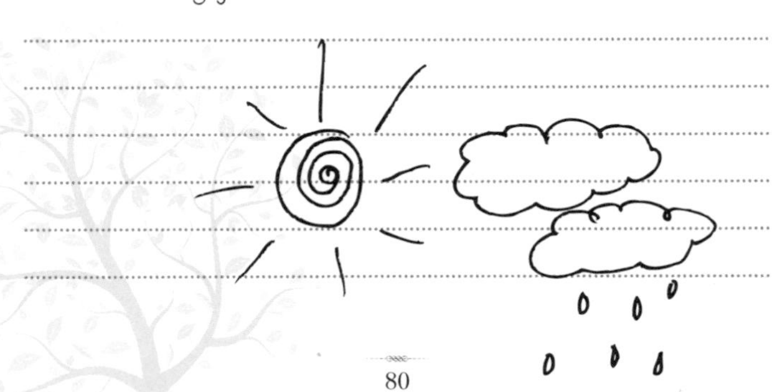

And looking back, I learned a lot. I didn't know that typhoons are the same thing as hurricanes. It just depends what side of the earth you are on.

I'm not going to tell you everything because I already put it in my paper, which had to be three pages. My parents read my paper and found lots of spelling mistakes. They helped me fix them and then I had to retype the whole thing over. My fingers were cramped up from all that typing.

The project took all day Sunday to complete and it put me in a bad mood. The only reason I didn't get really annoyed was that my mom said if I just buckled down and did the work without complaining, she'd agree to buy me a new dress I saw at the mall last weekend.

I can't wait to go shopping and get the dress! It's the most beautiful dress I've ever seen. It's pink with a belt. I can't wait to wear it and see if Paul notices.

Date: June 12

Dear Diary,

We got our research papers back today. I got a B plus. Miss Shannon wrote, "Good job" at the top. I was pretty happy, given the fact that I really am having a hard time concentrating with summer vacation just around the corner. When I showed the grade to my parents, they smiled and said they were proud of me. I'm so glad I don't have parents who are always saying, "Why didn't you get an A?" or, "Next time you had better get 100!"

Dorothy's parents are mean to her like that but she works really hard in school. She told me that sometimes she hides her report card because she knows her mom and dad are going to yell at her and maybe even hit her if she doesn't have all A's.

I might be young, but I know that's just not right. Parents should respect their kids and never put them down for not being the best student all the time. And they should never, ever hit them.

I feel really lucky that my parents don't yell at me about my schoolwork.

I wear my locket all the time. I love to touch it while I'm in school or on the bus ride home. It feels so good when I rub it with my fingers. I like to touch the engraving, too. It goes around and around in a circle that never seems to end.

I still don't have a second picture in it but I've decided it should be Paul who goes in there beside me. After all, he's the one I'm most in love with. I wonder how I can get Paul's picture, though? If I could have his picture in my locket it would be almost like we were really a couple.

Maybe, if I ask Angela nicely, she'll let me print one off from Facebook. Or maybe I could get his school picture, but I'd have to ask him for it and that might be a little embarrassing. And besides, it would be much too big for the locket. I'm not sure what to do! And school's almost over, so I better try to figure it out, and fast!

Date: June 17

Dear Diary,

How am I going to be able to deal with being at home all summer? Sometimes I can be so miserable at home. Usually it is when my parents start fighting. But if I can get away from them, then I'm okay. When I stay around and listen, I feel like they are yelling at me. But as soon as I get away then it's like I come alive again. Usually I just get on my bike or rollerblades or I walk down the hill to my friend's house, and then I feel okay.

I'm still sad for them and angry that they waste time fighting. But I guess I can really only control how I am going to feel. And leaving the house when they are fighting makes me feel better. So this summer, I'll just have to take control and do what makes me feel happy.

Date: June 21

candles

Dear Diary,

Today was the last day of school! These last few days have been really fun. Guess why. Miss Shannon got sick and we have the greatest substitute. His name is Mr. Reid and he's fun and also very nice. He told us he just finished becoming a teacher. I can't believe how different school has been. We made butter from milk by churning it by hand and then we ate the butter with crackers. We made candles with real string and melted wax. Mr. Reid also brought us all jump ropes and taught us how to exercise outside. He has a rule that we can't play anything where we choose sides until the last kid is chosen. When we asked why, he said, "Because it hurts feelings!" He actually said that! And he always calls on me when my hand is up. Five times so far he told me what a great answer I gave. Three times he said the question I asked was terrific. He made me feel so smart and good about myself. What a great way to end sixth grade!

I will never forget you, Mr. Reid! Thanks for making the end of the school year so much fun!

Date: June 24

Dear Diary,

I woke up this morning and realized that I won't be seeing Paul over the summer at all. I got up the courage to ask him what his plans were during the last week of school and he said he's going away to camp. Maybe he'll miss me? I know I'll miss him. I can't imagine him not being around and not seeing him every day at school. I feel lonely already. How will I get through each day?

I hate going to summer camp in the city. My parents always make me go and I have to drag my brother, too. Yuck. Twice a week the camp counselors make us swim in that awful "Y" pool that smells of chlorine, and they also try to teach us tennis. I hate tennis. I always miss the ball. And they have the most boring arts and crafts that we have to do. I don't want to make another wallet. What will I do with another wallet? I have five from last summer and besides, if I want to do crafts, there are plenty I can find online that are much more fun to make.

The more I think about it, the more this summer is going to be a huge drag.

Date: June 25

Dear Diary,

I just finished reading A Summer Camp Miracle Story. Angela said she loved the book so I borrowed it from her. In the story, Jackie goes away to camp and has all sorts of adventures, both bad and good. She wins an award for paddling a canoe the fastest and she makes lots of friends. But something bad happens. She almost drowns in the deep end of the lake. It's a long story. I don't even want to write all the details. It makes me feel so scared to even think about her struggling in the water. Finally she does get saved by the senior life guard and even has fun at the hospital getting treats and having her picture taken by the Waterville News, after having her lungs checked out because she swallowed so much water.

I don't think I should have read the book. It made me afraid of the water. I've always been a little afraid of swimming in deep water and now I'm really scared. I don't want to go to the beach this summer or to even swim in the pool at the Y. What am I going to do? Kids are supposed to love to go to the beach. Who can

I tell that I am petrified? I don't want to die by drowning!

I can't tell Angela. She'll think I'm a baby! I can't tell my mom, either. I know that she will tell me I'm being ridiculous and that I'm a good swimmer. And I can't tell my dad because he was so proud of me when I passed the intermediate swimming test.

It's times like this I don't know what to do. Am I being silly or should I find someone to confess this fear to?

Date: June 28

Dear Diary,

I can't wait to tell you what just happened! Remember how scared I was about swimming? Well, two days after I wrote that, my family went to Mountain Lake. My cousins also came in from Tremont—all five kids (Charlie is twelve, Karen is ten, Michael is seven, Patty is four, and Cindy is two) and Uncle Louie and Aunt Rita.

My mom made a giant picnic lunch to bring along. She got up early and fried chicken. It smelled so yummy. But then I had to peel all the potatoes for potato salad. That was okay (especially since I ate a bunch of chocolate chip cookies as I worked).

The lake was so beautiful and calm when we arrived. It was hot out, but not roasting. Really, the day was perfect. We were setting up the picnic lunch when suddenly Cindy ran into the water and disappeared under the surface. I guess there is a slope near the edge and she didn't know it. Everyone started to panic.

But guess who saved her? Yup, I did.

Without even thinking, I ran in and pulled her up by the back of her bathing suit. She was crying like crazy and kind of choking. Her mom came and scooped her up and hit her on the back so she spit up water. And soon she was okay and laughing while eating lunch with us.

So guess what? I'm not afraid of the water anymore. I went into the deep end just like I used to. After all, I am a good swimmer. I just got scared. Now, I feel so happy inside, like a big balloon filled inside me and I know I will always feel safe in the water.

Date: June 30

Dear Diary,

I wish I could travel to another country. I think it's so neat to meet new people, and seeing new things really is like getting a present.

I know when I grow up I'm going to travel a lot, and that's the truth.

The biggest trip I ever had so far was when we went to Florida in an airplane to the town where my Aunt Nelly lives. My aunt and uncle have a cute little ranch house. Of course, we had to stay with them, so I didn't have a chance to stay in a big hotel. I stayed in the finished basement, so I just pretended like I was a princess in my very own castle. That made not staying in a hotel a little better.

My parents let me go up in a tiny plane by myself (well, the pilot was there, too) while we were there. The County Fair was going on and it was one of the special rides you could buy a ticket for. The plane ride was wonderful. I was scared a little bit, and there wasn't even a roof on the plane. I was just sitting there behind the pilot with the wind pushing my hair into my eyes. My brother wanted to go too, but instead he got to go to the movies with my Aunt Nelly, as this was my special treat!

The pilot was so handsome. My heart was pounding from fright when the plane went really high. The pilot turned to me and said I could hold his hand if I was scared.

So guess what? While we were swooping over the houses and over the orange groves, I held his hand. It felt so reassuring and I also got the feeling of butterflies in my stomach. I wonder if he thought I looked older, maybe sixteen? Then we could maybe go out on a date.

When we finally landed, my parents were waving and throwing me kisses, and my mom looked like she had been crying. It was one of those really special moments when my mom and dad and I were all so happy together. They were happy I was alive and hadn't crashed, and I was happy I got to hold the pilot's hand and feel like I was sixteen.

It was a perfect day, and that's the truth.

Date: July 10

Dear Diary,

Angela, Betty, Joanne, Karen, Dorothy, Dawn, and I came up with a way to get through the boring summer. We meet at our houses once a week and trade books. It's like a club—a book trading club. That way we all get more books to read. We are trading all sorts of books and many of them I haven't read before.

Yesterday, we met at Dorothy's house. She has her own computer in her room, just like Angela. After we traded books, we watched music videos on YouTube and then practiced our own dance routines based on the various songs. We were laughing and having fun singing the songs and making up dances. Dorothy's mom finally came into the room and told us to settle down—that the whole house was shaking with us stomping around.

I had so much fun. Angela and I were still singing as we walked home.

Next week, we'll meet at my house. I'm going to bake brownies. Mom said she'll teach me the recipe she used when she baked brownies when she was twelve.

I'm really excited to show off my baking skills to my friends!

Date: July 12

Dear Diary,

I have been told that if you keep putting your face into expressions where you look mean and angry and irritated, your face is going to stay looking that way. If instead you keep smiling, laughing, and looking happy, then you'll stay looking more that way as you get older. I like the way Mrs. Hopkins down the street looks. She must be ancient, at least seventy or eighty-five like my great aunts. But she has this wonderful smile whenever she sees me that makes her face look so beautiful and even young! Her eyes sparkle and her voice sounds so warm like I am a very special person in her life. I want to be like her someday. Except her hair is white. I want to dye my hair a bright red when I get old—I saw a picture of an old lady online who had bright red hair and it looked incredible! And I'm always going to wear long earrings, lots of makeup, and big scarves and maybe even cowboy boots.

Date: July 13

Dear Diary,

I know a lot of truth about being healthy.

I feel good when I go for long bike rides and I stay outside a lot and I rollerblade. But when I'm sick I stay inside and rest. I have big tonsils. My mom told me I might have to have them out one day. I don't want to. She tried to make it sound like no big deal by telling me I would get to eat tons of ice cream after they take them out. But I'm scared about the pain and going under anesthesia. That's really what worries me the most. I hope they can stay right where they are and that I'll eventually stop getting sick because of them.

I read on a blog that eating healthy and getting lots of sleep are really important. Also taking the right vitamins is key to feeling good and having everything you need in your body to help you grow.

Health is one subject that my mom doesn't seem distracted when I bring it up. She is so into health foods and vitamins. She must have ten different bottles of pills she takes every morning. And she cooks most of our meals. We never have frozen dinners from the supermarket or pick up fast food. I'm happy that my mom is helping me stay strong and healthy. I hope that all this good food and vitamins means I won't need to have my tonsils out.

Date: July 15

Dear Diary,

I'm going to tell you the truth about friends and about knowing which people are good friends and which you should avoid.

Some people make you feel creeped out, and some always make you feel bad. The truth is you shouldn't hang around with those types of people. Some people make you feel wonderful, and those are the people you should be friends with. Angela makes me feel like that, and I consider her my best friend. I thought she wasn't when I saw her talking to Paul, but I believe her now. They were just working on schoolwork together. I feel bad that I got so jealous and wrote some mean things about her in here.

If you don't have anyone good to hang around with, then hang out with yourself! I know sometimes that's tough but it's better than being made to feel bad.

But Angela still might move and then I will have to make a new best friend. I like Dawn, but being at her house isn't as fun as being at Angela's. The rooms are so dark and the three dogs are always barking. And her older brother is kind of a bully. I'm afraid that even if I liked her as a best friend, her brother would make fun of me or bully me. I hope Angela doesn't move after all!

Date: July 19

Dear Diary,

I'm most happy when no one is fighting and no one is telling me what's wrong with me. I think that is the truth for just about everybody, and that's why I love being with my grandparents. We have a lot of fun and they don't ever criticize me. They like everything about me just the way I am. They even put that stupid picture of me, the one with my bangs cut off, up on the mantle and keep telling everyone how beautiful I am.

When my grandparents take me and my brother out, my mom stays home and rests. I'm really happy because we always have such a good time. They get us ice cream, and they take us to beautiful parks where we feed peanuts to the birds. One of the parks has rides and they let us go on them as many times as we want.

It's wonderful to be so happy.

And all it takes are people who love you, don't criticize you, and don't pick fights over anything.

And that's the truth!

Date: July 25

Dear Diary,

I've decided I love to eat delicious meals with people I care about.

When I'm with other people, I don't pig out like I do when I eat a giant Hershey bar alone in my bedroom. I sit up straight, mind my manners, and put my napkin in my lap. I pretend I'm a fancy lady in a large dining hall, like the ones I see in movies.

When I'm with my three great aunts, the stories they tell are amazing! They are really old, so I get to hear all about what it was like when they were kids: they lived in a big old Victorian house with three floors and a giant playroom that took up the whole third floor. It was filled with toys, books, and an old reed organ. They also told me how the trolley went right by their house and in the summer there was a different trolley that came by with straw seats and it was all open so you could get the breeze. No air conditioning! And they had only one phone in a closet under the stairway in the front hall. (They didn't even have computers back then! I was in shock!) The telephone didn't have a dial on it. When you had to make a call, you picked the receiver up and told the operator you wanted to make a call. Then the operator rang the person you wanted to talk to. But if you picked up the phone and heard someone else talking to a friend, you just had to hang up and check back later. There were only party lines in those days. That meant that up to four families shared the same line even though you had your own phone number. Can you imagine having to live like that?

I love hearing about the old days. I told Angela all about their stories and when I went over her house to sleep, we Googled images of all the things my great aunts talked about because our computer at my house is still broken. I wonder if my parents will ever fix it! We saw pictures of old telephones and old trolleys and old reed organs and even found big old Victorian houses just like the one they grew up in.

My great aunts always take me to the Sunshine Café for lunch. We order sandwiches, like egg salad, tuna, or cream cheese and olives, without the crusts. Then we get coffee Jell-O with whipped cream for dessert. Everything is so delicious. I eat while they chat about all sorts of things, like who died, when they are going to visit different relatives, and the next bridge game. I don't always listen; I just like to hear them talk. They always tell me how adorable I look and how pretty my haircut is and how smart I am.

The truth is being out with my great aunts is the very best way in the whole world to spend time during lunch.

Date: August 7

Dear Diary,

Our book trading club met at my house today. Thank goodness my brother was next door playing. He is such a pest. He probably would have ruined everything. I set the table in the dining room and my mom let me put Grandma's plates out for the brownies. We have six plates and they all have painted flowers on them. My mom said they came from Austria and they are very expensive. All the girls were very careful when using them.

The brownies I made were delicious. I ate four of them. Here's the recipe so I'll never forget it:

RECIPE

* 2 squares of unsweetened chocolate. (Yuck! Don't ever try to eat unsweetened chocolate plain. It is so bitter.)
* ½ cup Crisco
* 1¼ cups sugar
* 3 eggs
* ¾ cup flour

* ½ teaspoon baking powder
* ½ teaspoon salt
* ½ cup chopped nuts (optional) (I put in much more because I love nuts and no one has allergies to them)

First, I had to melt the chocolate over hot water (with Mom's help). Then, I mixed everything together and baked it for ½ hour at 350 degrees. I put coconut and colored sprinkles on top while the brownies cooled. (I made that part up.)

The book trading meeting was great. Everyone loved my brownies, too. We all traded books and talked about what we liked about them. Some of the girls talked about the latest vampire novels and others about teen romances they are reading. I told my friends about Nancy Drew. (None of them had even heard of these books but seem excited to read them now!)

My mom came into the dining room for a while and chatted with us, too. That made me feel so warm inside. And she told us about her favorite series growing up. She said that she started off reading the Bobbsey Twins. None of us had read that series (I didn't even know what this was). She said they were cute sets of twins, a boy and girl in each set, and they also solved mysteries. Maybe not as big as what Nancy Drew solves, but they were still smart. Maybe I'll try to find these books at the library. And when I'm at the library and can use the computer, I think I need to Google some other mystery books I might like. I'm sure there has got to be a lot out there that I don't know about!

Date: August 10

Dear Diary,

Only three more weeks until we go back to school. I had a nightmare last night that I couldn't find my new classroom. My heart was pounding in the dream and I was sweating a lot. I was running up and down the hallways. I knew I would be the last one to get to my new homeroom. No one comes in late on the first day! I was crying and then I was trying to move my legs in the dream, but I couldn't.

When I woke up, I was really sweating and my heart was beating fast. I went in to my mom and dad's room and lay down on the floor with a blanket from my bed. They didn't even know I was there. I just couldn't be alone after that dream. I hate dreams like that and that's the truth.

This morning, I told my parents about my bad dream. Mom said I had an anxiety dream and a lot of people do before they have to do something new. I'm glad she told me that. I hope I don't have any more anxiety dreams, though. They are no fun!

Mom told me a lot of other stuff today.

I guess it's because I'm getting older and she finally felt that I needed to know some things. And guess what. My mom really knows a lot, actually. She told me more about getting my period (our teacher told us a little bit about this last year in health class, but she filled in a lot of details). She told me I might get it any day. She said sometimes girls have lots of extra emotions as their bodies change. She said I might get in a bad mood more easily or cry at silly stuff but not to worry. She said there is plenty of stuff in the bathroom for me to use if I get my period when she isn't home.

I think that my mom should have been a doctor or a teacher. She never went to college but wants me to go.

She told me that she had a choice of being a secretary or working in my Uncle Dan's clothing store when she finished high school. She chose to become a secretary because my grandfather said he would pay for her to go to secretarial school.

I asked her if she had wanted to go to college. She said that she never thought about it because none of the girls in her family had ever gone to college. But now she wishes she had. She also told me that once my Uncle Tom said to her, "Edith, you are dumb but beautiful. Don't worry. That's okay. It is better than being dumb and not pretty."

Mom told me that she promised herself when I was born that I would get more education than she had. She told me that she has been putting ten dollars a week away since I was born for my college education. I was surprised and happy to hear this. It made me feel special to know that she was doing something just for me.

I hope I can make her proud of me when I get older. I know that I'm smart. I think I'm pretty. I also think what my uncle said to my mom was stupid. And I hope my mom knows how much I love her and think she's beautiful <u>and</u> smart.

Date: September 4

Dear Diary,

Tomorrow I go back to school. I'm excited and a little nervous as well. And for the first time in weeks, I thought about Paul. I know he's back home because I walked by his house and saw his bike in the driveway. I can't wait to see him. I wonder if he grew over the summer. I hope so. I think I still love him, but it's a little confusing since I haven't thought about him for a while now.

I try to remember his eyes and how they make me feel all funny inside, but it's a little tough. I guess I'll find out if I still love him tomorrow at school when I see him. Maybe I won't feel the same. I'm not so sure if I really love him anymore.

Date: September 5

Dear Diary,

The first day of school was pretty good. Our homeroom teacher is nice. Her name is Mrs. Gamble.

You won't believe this though: Paul is even shorter than I remembered! I guess I grew more over the summer than I realized. I didn't get the same kind of butterflies in my stomach when he walked into the room, either. I wonder what that means. I'm sitting in the same row he is, so it's harder to look at him all the time, because I have to turn my head. So maybe that's why? I'll have to keep investigating this, but for today, I just let it go.

And even better news is Angela told me she and her family have finally decided not to move after all. So I'm excited she is still here and also in my homeroom class!

And I've decided that I'm going to run for Student Council. The election will be in October. I'll have to make posters and give a little speech before the election. That's easy, though, as I like arty things and I also like speaking in front of people. I hope I win.

Date: September 11

Dear Diary,

Lately I get in bad moods a lot. Just like Mom told me I might! I'll probably get my period soon, too. I hope not. I hope it waits as long as possible.

The more I think about it, the more I don't really want to grow up yet. There are a lot of things I like about being my age. I can do a lot of things that grown-ups do, but I don't have their responsibilities or problems. I don't have to make money, and I don't have to involve myself in family troubles like my parents have to. They are always either fighting with each other or worried about the health of their parents or discussing money, and I don't have to do things like that—not yet. And I'm glad. That seems really tough.

I worry about my parents because they don't know the truth about so many things and they still fight over stupid stuff. They don't know how to have fun and how to stop arguing over things that never change. I don't think they really appreciate each other. No one is perfect. When will they ever grow up?

Date: September 18

Dear Diary,

Today is a day I will never forget. When I came out of the shower, I lifted my arm in front of the mirror as I was drying myself and I saw that I had three dark hairs growing from my right armpit! I can't believe it. It's beginning, just like Mom said. I'm not sure how I feel.

Good news: Nothing in the other armpit yet.

I don't want my body to change too fast. I'm used to myself, just the way I am. I like my legs and my hair and my eyes and I like still looking like a kid. An older kid, but a kid. I'm not ready to look like a teenager. I don't want to have to wear a bra after all. I don't want to get my period. I don't like the feeling of lipstick on my lips. I tried Angela's lipstick on at her house yesterday after school and it felt awful on my lips, like they were caked with food or something. I had to rush into the bathroom, get a Kleenex, and wipe it off. And I've decided I don't want to put makeup on my face—not yet. I also hate the smell of fresh nail polish. I wonder how much time I have left until I'll have to start doing all of these things, anyway. I can't believe I ever wished I could!

Date: September 19

Dear Diary,

Here's a little secret: when I wake up in the morning, I look at my wallpaper and try to see pictures in it that I have never seen before. There are flowers and birds, but sometimes I can see other things, like animals or faces. Doing that puts me in a good mood.

Then, before I get out of bed, I think of something good that will happen that day. I might get to watch my favorite TV show or play games on the computer (which finally got fixed over the summer—hurray!) or get to eat the chocolate cake left over from yesterday in the kitchen. As long as there is something that I know will make today a good day, I'm happy and that helps me enjoy the day that much more.

Even when I'm sick, I try to think of good things. I'll think about starting a new book or going shopping downtown with my friends. Even the day I threw up all day, I cheered myself up by lying on my parents' bed and reading a mystery book. I put pillows all around me and brought in my favorite doll. I felt sick, but I also felt nice and cozy.

There's always a way to make things better!

Date: October 5

Dear Diary,

There's a special song that sometimes floats into my head that is so uplifting: it gives me a funny feeling somewhere in my heart and stomach, like a magic tickle. I love it, but I don't know what it is and no one can identify it. It's as if I recognize it from a long time ago. Every once in a while, it comes back to me. It just enters my brain and I get that good feeling. I'm beginning to think I know that song from maybe before I was born.

I've tried to sing it aloud to lots of people, but no one recognizes it. I hope I can remember this song as I get older. The last time it came to me, my mom and I were walking downtown. She was taking me to get a new dress. I sang it for her, but she still didn't know it.

So this is really a puzzle, but it is still a truth that strange things can make us happy.

Date: October 10

Dear Diary,

I've been doing a lot of thinking and I definitely don't want to be a teenager. I don't want to obsess over makeup and clothes and flirting with boys.

I don't know if I want to go through all the stuff I read about in the teen magazine my cousin, Ruth, hides under her mattress. It has awful stories about breaking up with your boyfriend, and teenage girls who have babies but aren't married, and awful first kiss stories.

When I told my mom about the magazine, she just said not to "read that trash ever again." I won't, but I needed her to explain more about why those magazines exist. But she didn't say anything more—not about that or about growing up. I don't think she understands how frightened I am by it all.

I don't want to leave behind everything I know now and become some hysterical teenager!

Date: October 30

Dear Diary,

The most wonderful thing happened in school today. My class elected me to be their Student Council representative. I can't believe it! Five of us ran and I won. I was so scared when the teacher was counting the votes. I kept rubbing my locket for good luck. Then it turned out I got the most votes. When the teacher announced I was the winner, everyone clapped, even the losers. And Angela was one of the losers and she still came over and gave me a hug. She is a really good friend after all.

Now I get to go to the Student Council meetings once a week and help to make decisions about the school. I feel so grown up. The Student Council members will be deciding on lots of stuff like when we will have school dances and other really important things like school rules for the bathrooms. That may sound silly, but people do bad things in the bathrooms, like stand on the toilets and look at you when you pee. And some students have even been caught smoking in the bathrooms. I was so shocked the first time I smelled smoke in the girls' bathroom. I thought maybe there was a fire. And I also had two girls looking at me over the top of the stall when I went to the bathroom. That was a horrible—and embarrassing—experience. I hope we can make the bathrooms better.

We will also be discussing how to stop bullying in our school. It's not like we have a lot of bullies here, but there are a few and we want to make sure that kids at the school feel safe and aren't harassed. I'm hoping we'll be able to do something good to keep the other students safe and happy to be at school.

When I got home and told Mom I had won the election, she was really excited and gave me a huge hug. Then she told me to call and tell my grandma. When I did, she told me how proud she was of me. She said that maybe I will be governor of our state some day! She also said she is sending me a check for $20.00 as congratulations. I am very happy tonight. Maybe I will be (I mean governor someday)!

Date: November 14

Dear Diary,

I don't understand why teenage girls aren't more like adults or like the teenagers in my mystery books. Why must they go around laughing hysterically and being silly and wasting time? I'd rather be busy solving mysteries and helping people. I'd rather be curious and follow up on clues and take things seriously, but also have fun.

I don't get it. What happens to girls, like the ones who are older than me? Do they drink some kind of magic potion that makes them not have any brains? I hope I never drink that drink. I like my brain, and I like to feel smart.

I need help. I don't know who to turn to, though. My mom and dad? I don't think they can help me with the things I'm feeling. I just wish I had someone to talk to who would help answer my questions about being a teenager and reassure me that I won't be a ditzy, giggly, stupid girl when I turn thirteen next year.

The truth is, I'm afraid to ask my parents about this, so they really don't know I worry about these types of things. I don't know why I am afraid to talk about them. I just am.

Date: December 1

Dear Diary,

I have a secret. I am afraid of dying.

What happens to you when you die? Do you go somewhere else? Did I exist somewhere else before I was born? And how can I remember—after I die—all that happened to me when I was alive? What if it hurts to die? And what if I die too soon, before I can do all the things I want to do?

How can I stay alive forever?

I'm worried what will happen if my mom or dad or grandmother or grandfather die. I don't think I could stand it. I would go out of my mind. How can you go on living if people you love die? My parents and grandparents are the most important parts of my life. I can't even imagine existing without them.

I wish I had some way of knowing the answers to all of these questions. And I really wish I could figure out how to live forever—and then help my parents and grandparents to do the same.

R.I.P.

Date: December 5

Dear Diary,

Today I read the front page of the local newspaper when I brought it in from the lawn. My dad was waiting for me to bring it to him at the kitchen table. He called to me to hurry up. I was able to read just enough to upset me. The article I read was about a sixteen-year-old girl who tried to commit suicide. She was apparently recovering in the hospital, but was hooked up on a respirator, which I think is something that helps you breathe when you can't do it by yourself.

I feel really funny inside and scared, too. Reading the article just made me feel sick inside, like the Grand Canyon opened up in front of me and I couldn't stop moving forward. I don't even know this girl. I tried to check out more about her online but there wasn't much to be learned. But still, I can't get her out of my head.

Why would someone ever want to kill herself, especially someone who is only sixteen? Doesn't she have promises she made herself for the future? Maybe trying to make promises about the future don't work for some people, though? That scares me a lot, as I have so many things I want to do when I grow up, what I've promised myself I'll do when I'm older.

Maybe I can talk to Angela's mom about how this made me feel. But she might tell my mom and then my parents may be angry that I read the article or that I didn't talk to them first about it.

But I just want to live. I just want to understand! Someone help me!

Date: December 11

Dear Diary,

I've been carrying around those feelings of being scared—after reading that article in the paper—for a week now and finally, I decided to be brave. I told my mom how much the article about the girl in the newspaper upset me. She was leaning over the kitchen sink peeling potatoes for dinner when I told her.

She turned around and looked me directly in the eyes. Then she put down the peeler and wiped her hands on the dishcloth and put her arms around me. I wasn't expecting that. I started to cry like a plug had been pulled out of me and everything that scares me was draining out of my eyes through my tears.

Mom held me a long time and even brushed my hair back from my forehead and gave me tissues. She let me cry and only said, "I know how you feel."

Later, after I was done crying, she explained how sometimes people have very serious problems that others aren't aware of or don't know how to help them. Sometimes they have suffered extreme shock or losses or trauma.

They usually can be helped by the right doctors or by medicine. I shouldn't worry because she knows I am really a very normal kid and that she and Dad are here to make sure I have a safe and good life.

It was the best cry I've had in a long time. I guess my mom really does care about me.

Date: December 15

Dear Diary,

Tonight, Dad told me and my brother that he's been interviewing for a new job. If he gets it, we'll have to move away—not that far but far enough. I can't believe it. I won't see anyone I know again. Well, maybe that's a little dramatic, but at least I won't see people unless we make a really special effort to come back here, and I don't know if my parents will do that.

I guess the only positive thing about this is that Dad said we could get a bigger house and maybe even get a dog, too! But I think he's just saying that to make me not feel so strange about moving.

But I have this kind of scary feeling about leaving. I'm so used to my house, even the bushes that separate our house from our neighbors' house. I know where everything is and who everyone in town is, too.

Although I'm scared, I have to be brave and I'm willing to try new things. Of course it's going to be hard to leave Paul here. I'll never forget him, but if we're meant to be he'll find me! My mom keeps telling me that there'll be other boys. And you know what? I'm starting to finally believe her. I need someone to love me. Staring at Paul is not enough for me anymore. I need a boy who wants to stare back.

My mom also said that if Dad gets this new job, it will be really good for him and he'll get more money and people will look up to him. I think that's going to be good for him—for all of us. I think maybe my parents will fight less because my dad will feel better about himself. At least I hope so.

Even grown-ups have to feel good, or they get really cranky, and that's the truth.

Date: January 5

Dear Diary,

When I get older, will I still be me? Or will I have to do things that I don't want to do, like put all my dolls away and wear a bra? How will I feel about my body when I first get my period? (I don't even want to write the word, let alone say it aloud.) How will I still be me?

Another thing that most worries me is not knowing if the things I want to do in the future will actually happen. How can I make sure that my life will turn out how I want it to?

But, more importantly (at least for right now), I am worried about how I can get my parents to get me a pet. They keep saying no, not yet, whenever I ask, but they don't realize how sad this makes me. I really need something of my own to love.

Date: January 16

Dear Diary,

Angela told me <u>everything</u> about growing up when I slept over her house last Friday night. At least she said she told me everything she had learned from her mom. She invited me over on Wednesday and told me it would be a big secret-sharing night. I could hardly sleep the two nights leading up to it, just waiting. I had a feeling she was going to tell me a lot of stuff about growing up.

On Friday night, we had pizza for supper and checked our Facebook pages. I can only check mine when I'm at Angela's house, since our computer broke again. Ugh! Then we got into our pajamas and hid under the covers of her bed. We had to whisper and keep the light off so her mom would think we were asleep but it was hard to not giggle. Some things I knew, but lots I didn't. I felt okay about most of the stuff—like getting armpit hair, shaving my legs, having to wear a bra with an underwire, and what it might feel like to kiss a boy for the first time and how my stomach may go all tingly. We then opened her laptop (still under the covers) and did some online shopping for bras and razors and new clothes. Well, we just browsed, but I have a whole list of things I want to get soon.

After our talk, though, I still felt a little bit sad. I wish I could talk to my mom the way Angela can talk to her mom. I wish I could ask my mom all of these questions and get straight answers. I'm jealous of Angela because of this and told her so.

Angela said that at least it was time I ask my mom for a training bra. "It is never too soon," she said. Then she said her mom was going to get her one next week.

I guess Angela must have saw my chest when we got undressed and thinks I need to start wearing a bra.

I know I'm bigger than I used to be, but I'm scared to have to add this to my daily routine. And why do they call it a training bra anyway? What is there to train?

Date: February 6

Dear Diary,

Today, I was up in my room dancing to loud music on the radio. I was getting so hot and sweaty and really going wild. It felt great!

Then, all of a sudden, I saw Mom standing in the doorway. She had just come in without knocking! I thought she would get mad because my room was a mess and the music was so loud, and I'm sure I was making a lot of noise. But instead she just grinned. And you know what she did next? She started dancing with me! She even took a fake long-stemmed rose and held it between her teeth, like they do in movies when a woman is dancing the tango. And you know what? She actually knows how to dance! I couldn't believe it. It was the first time I've ever seen my mom dance and she is really good!

We danced like crazy for two more songs. Then she collapsed onto my bed and pulled me down with her, scooping me up in a big hug. She looked happier than I've seen her in a long time. She told me that she used to dance in her bedroom when she was a kid, and she would hold her hairbrush in her hand like a microphone and pretend to sing. Imagining her doing that made me laugh like crazy.

I was so happy today. I hope we dance together again soon.

☺

Date: February 12

Dear Diary,

I figured out a way to not get so angry when I have lots of homework to do and I don't feel like working on it. Here is my new plan:

* Come home and have a snack.
* Get right to work on any assignments and work for half an hour.
* Take a break and read a chapter of my library book (fun reading!).
* Work for another fifteen minutes.
* Play Candy Crush on Mom's phone.
* Do more homework for another fifteen minutes.
* Go outside and take a bike ride or if the weather is nasty I call one of my friends.
* Eat supper.
* Do more homework.
* Have dessert.
* Finish any remaining homework.
* Take a shower and watch TV, then go to bed.

And that's it. That is my whole night.

It is a great way to do things because I discovered with all these breaks I usually finish all my homework or I can figure out what I can leave for another night. And I don't feel like it's such a burden to have to get done. And then I actually don't mind having to do the homework because I know I'll get to do other things I really enjoy.

Things are so much easier when I'm not in a horrible mood and that's the truth!

Date: February 20

Dear Diary,

I'm at least four inches taller than Paul now. I'm guessing, but I can tell you I am at least three inches taller and maybe five! That bothers me. Even though I'm pretty sure he doesn't see me as girlfriend material, I still like him. But for some reason, I feel less attracted to him now that he's so much shorter.

Gotta run. Mom's calling me for dinner.

Date: February 22

Dear Diary,

So it's final. My dad got the new job. He told me, Mom, and my brother at dinner. We'll be moving in June. I tried to act excited but I felt sort of numb when he told us.

I think Mom might have seen the look on my face because she said we can come back and visit all my friends, because we're only moving thirty miles away. I tried to smile but I think it looked more like a grimace. I left the table without asking for dessert.

My life won't be the same. Ever.

Date: March 1

Dear Diary,

You're not going to believe this. I walked into the living room and Dad was sitting on the couch, crying. He told me that my uncle (his brother) was sick and had to have a very serious operation. He was very worried. I asked Dad if Uncle Dave is going to die and he said he wasn't sure, but it didn't look good. Mom walked in then and it looked like she had also been crying. Seeing both of them so upset made me feel so funny and scared inside, like a big giant pit was opening up at the bottom of my stomach.

Dad is scared and Mom is upset and now I'm both scared and upset. I love my Uncle Dave. He's always been so good to me. He brings me treats when he visits and he took me horseback riding a couple of times. I need him to get better!

Date: March 7

Dear Diary,

Well, I've decided that I don't care that Paul is so short. This must be true love because it has lasted so long, even with him being shorter than I am and even with some of my doubts about whether he likes me or not. But I have to admit I'm getting discouraged.

I really hoped even though Paul's a boy, and my mom says that boys don't fall in love and that they don't even care about girls, that he would be different. I keep hoping that he will show his love for me, and soon.

The pain is so immense I want to die—except if I die now, I'll never get a dog, and Mom hinted I might be getting one when we move. She almost promised when I told her I felt so funny about moving. She said that was normal.

I don't like that part of being normal.

Date: March 16

Dear Diary,

My cousin Eddie isn't in college anymore. My parents were all upset yesterday because they got a call from my Aunt Lil saying that Eddie was expelled from college. She was crying so hard on the phone that my dad had to keep telling her that it would be alright and just take a deep breath and get a drink of water.

I was eating breakfast and eavesdropping on the conversation at the same time. I heard my dad also tell Aunt Lil that Eddie could probably go back to school but after he was "clean." That part didn't make any sense to me. Did Eddie get kicked out of college because he didn't shower often?

After Dad left for work, I asked Mom what it meant that Eddie wasn't "clean." She said that Eddie was caught taking drugs—not the kind that you take when you have a headache but drugs that aren't legal. She said Eddie was swallowing stuff in his room that could have made him very sick and that he was giving it to other kids in the dorm. The dean of his college found out and made him leave. My aunt is trying to find help for Eddie so he won't do bad stuff anymore. That's what my dad meant by getting "clean." It means not using illegal drugs anymore.

I know what drugs are—a police officer came to school once to tell us about them and that we should never use them. But I never knew anyone who took any.

I've been thinking about Eddie all day. When we go to visit my aunt and uncle once a year, I always play cards with him. He is seven years older than I am, but I still liked playing with him and he never teased me. He was always so nice to me.

It is sad and scary what happened to him. I'm not sure I want to see him again this year when we go to their house. And that's the truth.

Date: March 30

Dear Diary,

Today was my birthday! I can't believe I am thirteen.

13

It sounds so old. I forgot to tell you that Aunt Belinda sent me another birthday package last week. I hid it in my underwear drawer, just like last year. After we came back from dinner at the steak house in town (that was part of my present from my parents), I opened all my presents. Aunt Belinda sent me a birthstone ring. It is so beautiful—the stone is sea-green and the setting is real gold. Inside the band she inscribed: "Love you!" and I could see 10k also etched in there. The ring must have cost so much. I love her, too. Mom and Dad gave me a gift card for clothes and also a note promising me a plane trip all by myself to visit

Aunt Belinda. I guess they realize I really am growing up. But what about the puppy? I still need a dog to love.

Grandma gave me money and a beautiful pink fluffy bathrobe and slippers to match. My brother gave me a list of promises inside a birthday card he made. He promises to 1) rub my back anytime I want, 2) clean up my room for me twice during the year, 3) help take care of my dog (maybe he knows something I don't?), and 4) not bother me when I'm doing homework.

I forgot to tell you, too, that Angela came with us to dinner and back to the house after for cake and presents. She laughed so much as my brother read his promises aloud. He was so sincere. I gave him a big hug and kiss. Angela gave me an ankle bracelet. It is beautiful with a tiny gold heart on it. I'm so lucky to have such a good friend.

Date: April 3

Dear Diary,

Paul behaves like I'm not even there. Do you think I stare at him too much? Oh, Paul, look at me, love me. I am sitting right near you totally in love! And tonight when I lie in bed I'll be imagining us getting older and being boyfriend and girlfriend for real.

I still wear my locket all the time. I never did put Paul's picture in it, though.

I'm miserable.

Date: April 23

Dear Diary,

I don't think I am going to be able to be a dancer when I grow up. The girls that are really good in ballet/tap/jazz and acrobatics can do all sorts of things I can't do, even though I try. Gloria is still better than almost everyone in our class. She can spin four or five times around on one turn and she doesn't ever fall. I can only go around once. And most of the girls can do full splits. I can't. I think there is something wrong with my body. It just doesn't want to do what I want it to do.

Last night was my dance recital. I think this might be my last. I felt really fat in my costume, and I made a couple of mistakes on the stage. I don't know if anyone else noticed, but I did.

The recital was in our school auditorium. First, I thought I looked good in my lobster costume for the Bottom of the Sea Ballet, but then I thought I looked stupid when I saw myself from the side. I looked fat.

My parents said the dance routine was very hard and they were impressed with how I did.

My mom said that no one saw me trip. I asked my brother if he saw me make any mistakes and he said he didn't. But I just realized that he probably wasn't even watching the stage, and I'm sure my mom told me no one saw my mistake just to make me feel better. Oh, this is terrible. I'm fat and I think my dream to be a ballet dancer has been crushed . . . and that's the truth.

Date: May 12

Dear Diary,

We had Career Day at school today. It was a lot of fun! Our class has been preparing for it for few weeks now. We had to pick three careers that we wanted to find out more about from a long list our teacher gave us. Then on career day all these grown-ups come to school and we had meetings with them.

I picked these three careers to learn more about:

1. Detective
2. Dancer
3. Writer

It was fun getting ready for Career Day, too. I got to read all about famous detectives like Sherlock Holmes and Dick Tracey. I also read about some of the famous ballerinas, like Pavlova, and other famous dancers like Isadora Duncan, who started Modern Dance. And I read about famous writers like Leo Tolstoy and William Shakespeare.

Oh, I forgot to tell you that we dressed up

like we were already in one of our professions for Career Day, too. I dressed up like a detective, since that was my number one career choice. I wore a nice suit and carried a purse with a magnifying glass in it and a pair of handcuffs and a notepad to take notes.

I enjoyed all three speakers, but they made me worry. It is hard to be a detective. You have to work for years before you get the license.

It is hard to be a dancer, too. You have to practice hours a day for years. And I'm probably too fat already to be a dancer.

It is hard to be a writer—you have to write every day.

I hope I can pick the right profession and I hope I can work hard enough when the time comes. But what if I can't? What will happen to me?

I do enjoy writing to you about my day and my feelings and what's going on in my life. So maybe I <u>will</u> become a writer when I grow up. I guess that could be kind of cool.

Date: May 28

Dear Diary,

Angela, Dorothy, and all of the other girls threw me a special party today at Betty's at our last club meeting, since I'll be moving next month. They all brought me gifts, which was really nice.

Dorothy brought me a beautiful diary to write in. Maybe I'll use it when we move or when I've written on every page of this diary. Angela gave me a gift certificate to the bookstore in my new town. Her mom must have driven her there to get it. I think that was especially sweet. Dawn gave me a bracelet with a heart that is engraved with my name. I can wear it when I wear my locket.

Betty's mom made us dinner. We had macaroni and tuna casserole, peas, and homemade apple pie. Then we had peanut butter cups, four each. I love the way peanut butter cups feel in my mouth. Betty's mom is the best. I'll never forget today. Before we all left, Betty's mom also took a group picture and said she'd email it to my mom so we can print and frame it.

I wonder if I'll really see all the girls again after I move. I hope so. It's going to be hard leaving all my friends behind. And I wonder if I'll be able to start another club in my new town, with my new friends.

Date: June 7

Dear Diary,

I was watching a show on TV that was about a mom who stays home with her kids all day and what that is like. I've decided that I don't want to stay home during the day when I grow up. I want to have a career. I'm not going to let anybody trap me inside a house with nothing to do but chores and laundry.

To get a career, I'll have to get the right kind of education. If I'm going to be an actress then I'll get training at an acting school. If I'm going to be something else, I'll do whatever it takes to make sure I meet my goals. I just know that I don't want to be stuck at home with my kids forever.

I'm going to be somebody out in the world. And that's the truth.

Date: June 12

Dear Diary,

My mom just told me that she is expecting a baby in five months.

I can't believe it!

I am not happy at all!

As much as my little brother bugs me, we have sort of worked out a system and can at least get along most of the time. But we certainly don't need to share our house or things with anyone else or to take care of a baby! And we are moving, too. I'll have so much on my mind: a new school, a new house, and new friends. I thought I would have enough to worry about having to take care of a new dog (hopefully). Now, I'll have to listen to a baby crying at night, change dirty diapers, and all of that!

This is just not fair!

Date: June 21

Dear Diary,

Next week we're moving.

I've been packing like crazy. My parents don't know how to pack, but I do, so I've kind of been in charge. Mom said she didn't know what they'd do without me and my good packing skills. And it's true: I'm good at figuring out how to get lots of things into one box. Most of our things are in boxes now. I'm kind of excited, and I'm also kind of scared.

I went on a bike ride around the neighborhood today. I looked at the big tree that I always climb in the neighbor's yard, and I said goodbye to it. I rode to the drugstore and had maybe my last coffee ice cream cone. I rode down the hill really, really fast one last time. I even went to the other end of the street where I usually don't go, just so I can remember all the houses for the entire four blocks that are our street.

The best thing about moving, though, is our new house. You should see it! It's bigger than the one we live in now and it's all one floor with three bathrooms! I never thought we'd live in a house with three bathrooms! It has a back porch and a big yard. The last family who lived there left a swing set so my brother and I can swing there instead of at a park. It's in a very pretty neighborhood. I'll be turning fourteen in my new house with my new friends and everything. That's a long time away. I just hope I have new friends by that time. . . .

Date: June 22

Dear Diary,

I can't believe I forgot to tell you that we had our school dance at the end of the year and Paul asked me to dance—twice! He didn't ask anyone else to dance more than once, so I was very happy.

It was funny dancing with him, though, since he's so much shorter than I am. I couldn't even look into his eyes. I just looked over his head, across the gym to the wall. But I still felt a little tingling in my body being that close to him. I don't think I'll put his picture in my locket now, though, especially since I'll be moving and will probably never see him again.

I'm not sure what I'll put in there.

Date: June 23

Dear Diary,

I'm not as scared of getting older now for some reason. I don't know why exactly. I wasn't even upset when I lifted my arms in front of the mirror recently and saw too many hairs to bother to count them—in both armpits now, too. I guess I'll need to find a YouTube video that will teach me how to shave my armpits. Or maybe I could ask my mom.

I feel a little rush of excitement when I think about moving and making new friends and growing up. It's different than the feeling I felt when I thought I was in love with Paul. This time, it's just an overall good feeling.

I've decided that when we move I'm not going to set up all my dolls on the dresser. I'm going to put some of them away carefully in boxes along with their clothes. I'm also not going to take all of my comic books to the new house. I've begun to sort through them. I'm giving away the ones for kids and only keeping the ones I've really enjoyed reading over and over again.

Well, maybe I'll keep one of my favorites that's for kids. Just to remember.

Date: June 26

Dear Diary,

I wonder if I'll be able to sleep tonight.

The movers are coming at 8:00 tomorrow morning!

Since I am having trouble falling asleep, I've made a list of what I wish and hope for:

I hope our move is safe and good and we'll all be happy in our new house.

I hope my parents will fight less.

I hope I remember forever the truth, even when I grow up.

I hope when I have children, our house is filled with laughter and fun.

When my kids ask me questions, I hope I tell them the truth.

I hope I remember to never forget the tiny things, like licking the salt off my skin after I sweat.

I hope I remember how to dress and how to keep my face looking soft.

I hope I can become a teenager without being too afraid.

I hope I will not feel too bad about leaving behind what I have to leave behind.

Date: June 27

Dear Diary,

The movers are coming in twenty minutes! I am so excited I can hardly sit still, let alone think straight!

I finally decided what I want to put into my locket. I'm putting a tiny slip of paper that has on it the things I don't want to forget about myself. I might have to write in code because it is so small. But I'll know how to break the code. That's because I'm smart—just like a detective.

I decided my secret reminder is more important than a picture of Paul. I'll never forget him, of course, but the secret I'm putting inside the locket is for me, forever. I'll wear my locket next to my heart, so I'll always remember what's important to me. The words will face my face when the locket is closed, so I'll always remember the truth.

Date:

Dear Diary,

Things I promise to do when I grow up:

* I'll travel a lot.
* I won't look away when my kids ask me tough questions.
* I'll answer questions truthfully.
* I won't swear.
* I won't get into silly fights with other people.
* I'll have fun with my kids and laugh a lot.
* I'll remember ME!

And that's the truth!

Questions for Kids

1. What do you think happens right after the book ends?
2. What do you think about the girl in *The Truth*?
3. What did you like about her?
4. What didn't you like?
5. Have you ever felt like her?
6. Did she teach you anything?
7. Do you know anyone like the girl in the book? If so, what is she like?
8. Would you like to have a friend like the girl in the book?
9. What would you like to tell the girl if she were real?
10. What do you think the girl would say to you?
11. Are there any secrets you would tell the girl?
12. Do you think the girl had other secrets that she didn't put in her diary?
13. How is she different from you?
14. How is she the same as you?
15. What was your favorite entry from her diary?
16. What was the funniest part of *The Truth*?
17. Are there important things the girl didn't talk about that you thought she should have?

18. What made you angry in the book? Sad? Happy?
19. What do you want to remember most when you grow up?
20. What do you wish your parents better understood about you?
21. Would you like your mom and/or dad to read this book?
22. Is there a part of *The Truth* that you would like to talk to your mom or dad about?
23. If you could give the girl a name, what would you name her?
24. Would you like to write to the girl? If you would like to write to her, here is the address to use: drbarbara@enchantedself.com

About the Author

Dr. Barbara Becker Holstein, nationally known positive psychologist, is the creator of The Enchanted Self,® a systematic way of helping bring more joy, meaning, and purpose into our lives.

Dr. Holstein has been a school psychologist for more than twenty-five years. She also taught first and second grades. She is in private practice as a psychologist, with her husband, Dr. Russell M. Holstein, in Long Branch, New Jersey.

You can find Dr. Holstein on the web at www.enchantedself.com, at *The Truth* blog at www.thetruthforgirls.com, on Facebook at www.facebook.com/thetruthforgirls, and you can write to her at drbarbara@enchantedself.com.